MASTER OF THE BEASTS

DOOMSKULL
THE KING OF FEAR

With special thanks to Troon Harrison
To Marek Ewing

www.beastquest.co.uk

ORCHARD BOOKS
338 Euston Road, London NW1 3BH
Orchard Books Australia
Level 17/207 Kent St, Sydney, NSW 2000

A Paperback Original
First published in Great Britain in 2012

Beast Quest is a registered trademark of Beast Quest Limited
Series created by Beast Quest Limited, London

Text © Beast Quest Limited 2012
Inside illustrations by Pulsar Estudio (Beehive Illustration)
Cover illustration by Steve Sims © Beast Quest Limited 2012

A CIP catalogue record for this book is available from
the British Library.

ISBN 978 1 40831 523 1

5 7 9 10 8 6 4

Printed and bound by CPI Group (UK) Ltd, Croydon, CR0 4YY

Orchard Books is a division of Hachette Children's Books,
an Hachette UK company

www.hachette.co.uk

DOOMSKULL
THE KING OF FEAR

BY ADAM BLADE

ORCHARD

So... You still wish to follow Tom on his Beast Quest.

Turn back now. A great evil lurks beneath Avantia's earth, waiting to arise and conquer the kingdom with violence and rage. Six Beasts with the hearts of Ancient Warriors, at the mercy of the Evil Wizard, Malvel, who I fear has reached the height of his powers.

War awaits us all.

I beg you, again, close this book and turn away. Evil will rise. Darkness will fall.

Your friend,
Wizard Aduro

PROLOGUE

Daltec threw an apple into the air. "Watch this!" he said gleefully to King Hugo, who walked at his side. With a muttered spell, Daltec cast a hand over the apple and with a *chirp* it turned into a sparrow. The little bird fluttered away into the orchard.

"It was supposed to turn into an eagle!" Daltec grumbled.

"Never mind that," King Hugo said. "Tell me about the battle against the Beast of the Icy North. Have you seen anything in Aduro's crystal ball?"

Daltec, the youngest apprentice to the Wizard Aduro, ran a hand through his curly hair. "My King," he said with a bow, "I have not looked in the ball yet this morning."

"Too busy with your studies, hmm?" asked King Hugo.

Daltec's face flushed. "I was— I was—"

"In the kitchen eating pastries," said King Hugo. "Pay attention, Daltec. I have never known our kingdom of Avantia to be in such great peril. If the Evil Wizard Malvel returns here, all could be lost. *All*. Do you understand?"

They were in the royal gardens and the king's gaze ran over the trees, which were covered in red, orange and yellow fruit. The domes and spires of the palace rose all around them. Beyond spread Avantia. The land was protected by six legendary Beasts, though few people knew of their existence. Usually, this was enough to keep the kingdom safe, but the Evil Wizard Malvel had raised six good knights from the dead and turned them into wicked, deadly Beasts.

King Hugo walked on. "I hope Taladon the Swift is safe. I'm counting on him to help Tom protect Avantia."

"Perhaps Aduro will soon send word of victory," Daltec suggested. "I'll run and look into the crystal ball. Maybe the heroes are already returning after slaying Tecton the Armoured Giant!"

"Do not underestimate Malvel," King Hugo warned. "He's turned six good knights into Evil Beasts – who knows what more he's capable of? Go now and find out about the battle in the Icy North."

"I'll go at once," the apprentice said. He closed his eyes and spun around three times, mumbling. When he reopened his eyes, he was not in Aduro's chamber as he had hoped. Instead, he was lodged in the branches of an apple tree less than ten strides away from where he had been standing.

"I need to practise that spell more," he said sheepishly.

The king waved his hand. "Be off with you!"

Daltec scrambled down and loped away.

Hugo continued his walk through the orchard. Fear weighed him down. His shoulders slumped and his forehead creased. "Why has no word come from the north? All could be lost," he muttered.

Movement caught the king's eye. Was it a peacock? Or a deer? No, light glinted off something golden. Golden armour! King Hugo's eyes lit up.

"Taladon!" King Hugo cried in welcome. "Do you have news of victory?"

The knight pushed back his visor with a gauntleted hand. King Hugo faltered. Had the battle in the north changed the face of his Master of the Beasts so much? Where was Taladon's golden beard? This knight had a clean-shaven face. A cunning smile revealed a chipped tooth. It was not Taladon the Swift standing before the king.

King Hugo's hand fell to where his

sword belt was usually fastened,
but today, he was not wearing it.

"Halt!" the king cried. "State your
name!"

The Golden Knight stepped closer.

"Do not strike me, for I am
unarmed," King Hugo said. "I will
fight you in fair combat. Honour
demands that we both be armed
before we duel."

The knight made no reply. Light
rippled on his golden armour. Was it
moving? King Hugo's eyes widened
in panic. Something was wrong. The
knight's armour wavered and heaved.
He was turning to golden stone!
Flames flickered around his neck and
became a blazing mane. King Hugo
flung up a hand to ward off the heat.
Now the knight's eyes glowed like
craters. A skeletal muzzle replaced

the cunning face. From the bones
sprouted curved, sabre-tooth fangs.

The Beast crouched to spring.

"Get back! I am King Hugo of
Avan—"

The king's words ended in a shout
of pain and terror.

CHAPTER ONE

A CAPTURED KING

The ground jolted beneath Tom's feet. Everything whirled around him: the palace turrets, blue skies, chickens. *Chickens*? Tom staggered and regained his balance. He looked around to see where Aduro's magic had brought him. "The courtyard of King Hugo's palace," he said in relief. The Good Wizard had used his magic to bring them back from Avantia's icy plains

where they had battled the Beast
Tecton.

"I've never been so happy to see
it," gasped Elenna, appearing at
his side. She pushed back her dark
hair. "Silver!" she called as her wolf
appeared, scattering the chickens
again. Storm, Tom's black stallion,
struck the cobblestones with a ring
of his horseshoes.

"Here we are then, safely back,"
pronounced Aduro the Good Wizard
as he too appeared in the courtyard.

"Don't be alarmed," Tom cried to
the courtiers who had scrambled
away with shouts of fear. Reassured,
the people pressed forward, eager
for news.

"What news do you bring from the
Icy North?" cried a man.

"Why are you wearing…?" another

man started to ask Tom. "Isn't that Taladon's Golden Armour?"

At these words, Tom stood as though frozen in place. He felt numb with misery.

"Where is our Master of the Beasts?" another man demanded.

Still Tom could not speak.

"Taladon is no longer with us," Elenna said. "He is… He died at the hand of the White Knight." Tears streaked her face.

The courtiers let out a groan of dismay.

"No, I cannot believe it," muttered Captain Harkman, head of the King's personal guard. "Such a hero cannot be beaten. And we were so close to victory!" Five of the six knights had been defeated – there was only one more Quest to go.

One Quest too late, Tom thought. *My father will never be able to join in the fight.* Taladon had perished on the icy plains, killed by the White Knight's lance.

Aduro laid a hand on Captain Harkman's arm. The wizard was stooped with grief. "Alas, Elenna speaks the truth," he said. "Already, the body of Taladon the Swift lies here in the palace crypt. Go and pay your last respects to a loyal servant of Avantia."

The crowd drew back, faces taut with fear. With a heavy tread, Captain Harkman led them away towards the crypt.

My father's blood is on my hands, Tom thought through the fog of grief. He turned towards the horse trough, pulled off Taladon's golden helmet and carefully placed it on a stone. In the dark water his reflection shimmered. Taladon's armour, though scratched and dented, still gleamed. *Now I possess all the Armour's special abilities,* Tom thought. *But I feel like an impostor.*

He looked over at Elenna. "I'll never be a hero like my father," he said, the words choking him. "I let him die. I've let everyone down."

"Tom, you mustn't torment yourself," Elenna said gently, taking his arm. "Your father died proud of you for taking up the Quest."

"I must give the bad news to King Hugo, and beg his forgiveness," Tom said.

Tom headed for the throne room. Captain Harkman appeared at his shoulder but Tom ignored him.

After one look at Tom's grim face, the captain stood aside. Tom's feet dragged over the tiles. *How can I bring such terrible news to my King?* he wondered. When he reached the throne room, it was silent. Hugo's gilded chair stood empty in a shaft of sunlight.

Tom turned and ran up the stone steps to Aduro's chamber.

"Is King Hugo here?" he demanded, peering inside.

The apprentice, Daltec, shot Tom a startled glance. "There's no one here but me," he replied.

Tom marched back down the stairs. "You!" he called to a servant passing in the hallway. "Where is King Hugo?"

The boy paused, straining to hold onto the basket of ripe fruit he was taking to the kitchen. "I just saw him in the orchard talking to Taladon."

"Taladon?" Tom snapped. "*Taladon*? Is that some sort of joke?" He lunged towards the boy and grabbed him by his tunic. "How dare you joke about my father?"

"N-no joke," the servant stuttered. "I j-just saw our king talking to a knight in golden armour among the apple trees."

The Golden Knight from the Gallery of Tombs. A jolt of energy shot through Tom. *He's attacking us here, in the palace!*

He let the servant go and bolted down the hallway and out of the arched door. "Elenna! Aduro!" Tom cried, seeing the two trudging across the courtyard. "We must go to the orchard. King Hugo is in danger from the Golden Knight!"

"Not the King, too," moaned Aduro. They ran after Tom, their feet pounding the ground as they sprinted through the long swathes of grass between the trees.

"Look, the grass has been trampled here!" Aduro cried. Bending, Tom saw the gouges in the ground, as though a fight had taken place.

"There are drops of blood leading

away from the palace!" Elenna cried.

They hurried along the faint trail of red spots. "It's leading us to the rear wall of the castle grounds," Tom said. He laid one hand on the hilt of his sword. He stumbled to a halt and Aduro and Elenna paused beside him. All three of them stared at the line of blood spots.

"It's disappeared!" Elenna gasped. "It just stops."

"But here's King Hugo's clasp." Tom bent and picked up the golden pin that fastened the king's cloak.

"The king has been taken!" Aduro wailed.

"Tom, catch him!" Elenna said. But he was too late. With a moan of horror, the old wizard buckled at the knees and fainted to the ground.

CHAPTER TWO

CHAOS IN THE CASTLE

"Nothing we could do… Too late. Malvel always said he'd win… Too late. Where's my young apprentice? I must tell him important things. Taladon, oh Taladon!"

Aduro lay on a bed in the castle infirmary. Tom listened in dismay. *I've never seen Aduro like this before,* Tom thought. His stomach curdled with fear.

"Why is he like this?" Tom asked.

"He's suffering from terrible shock," replied the king's own physician as he wiped Aduro's sweating face with a damp cloth.

Tom gripped the wizard's shoulders. "Aduro," he said fiercely. "Stop this moaning. We must track the Golden Knight before he harms our king!"

"Apple pie," mumbled the wizard. "Must tell Daltec. Too late."

"Aduro!" Tom shouted. "Stop this! We need you!"

"Let him go, Tom. You will do him further harm," the physician warned. "He is gravely ill."

At the side of the bed, Silver whined uneasily and the hackles lifted on his back. Elenna pulled Tom away from Aduro's twitching body. "Tom," she said urgently. "Look at

me. We can't waste any time. We
must leave Aduro here and fight on."

"I'm not strong enough," Tom said.
He felt broken. "I can't face this battle
on my own."

"You're not on your own," Elenna
said gently. "I am here and so is
Silver, and Storm awaits in the
stables. Together we can battle the
cursed knight."

Shouts echoed down the hallway
to the infirmary.

"Hush! What is this new
commotion?" asked the physician.

Tom lifted his head to listen, and
Silver prowled to the door with his
ears pricked up.

"Perhaps the Golden Knight has
returned!" Elenna gasped.

Tom's hand flew to his sword and
he raced through the servants' narrow

corridors. Elenna and Silver were close behind. The screams seemed to be coming from the kitchen. Tom burst into the large room and skidded to a halt by a fireplace. Breathing hard, he stared around.

Iron cauldrons, silver platters and spilled food lay strewn over every surface. Apple sauce smeared the floor. Cooks and serving girls huddled in one corner clutching forks and rolling pins.

Tom's nostrils wrinkled at the foul stench. "Varkule!" he said. Varkules were the knights' foul creatures. Tom's eyes scanned the kitchen. *There!* The snarling beast lurked in a corner behind a clay water pot. Tom drew his sword. At his side, Elenna notched an arrow to her bow. Shoulder to shoulder they stepped towards the fearsome animal. At any moment, it could spring into an attack.

"What's it doing here?" Elenna asked.

"I don't know," Tom said.

He kept a tight grip on his sword as the Varkule lay down on the tiles

like a dog. It licked its leathery paws. There was a long moment of silence as the cooks watched in terror.

"What's it wearing around its neck?" Tom said. "I'm going to take a closer look. Cover me with your bow and arrow."

Elenna nodded and held her bowstring taut. Cautiously, Tom advanced one step at a time with his sword held out.

"Leave the kitchen! Get to safety," Tom called over his shoulder to the kitchen servants. He continued to advance. Now he was close enough to see that the thing around the Varkule's neck was a leather thong from which hung a glass bottle. Was the varkule carrying a message from the Golden Knight?

Holding his breath, Tom stooped closer. The Varkule's lips wrinkled

back over its fangs but it did not
move. Tom reached out a hand,
willing his fingers to stop trembling.
The Varkule didn't lunge or attack.
It wants me to take the glass. He reached
further and untied the leather thong
that held the phial while the Varkule
glared with its red eyes. Tom lifted the
phial and retreated back to Elenna.

He pulled the cork stopper from
the neck of the bottle. A blue mist
shimmered out into the air. It swirled
until an image appeared.

"It's the Golden Knight!" Elenna
gasped.

Inside the mist, the image of the
knight shone brightly. Light glinted
on the two forked daggers he held,
one in each hand. His visor was up
so that Tom could see his face.

"He has King Hugo," Tom muttered.

The knight grinned, revealing a chipped tooth. He pressed the edges of the forked daggers against the king's throat. Hugo's eyes bulged with terror.

The familiar voice of Malvel made the hair stand up on Tom's neck. It echoed through the air, sent by evil magic. "I'm close, so close," Malvel said. "So very nearly in your kingdom. But my magic needs a

little extra…help." He let out an evil laugh. "A simple choice lies before you, Tom. Persuade Aduro to help me break back into Avantia. If you don't I will instruct my Golden Knight to slay King Hugo. What do you say, Tom? You really have no choice. You can't want your king, as well as your father, to die. I expect to be back in Avantia by nightfall."

"You don't understand – Aduro's senseless! I can't persuade him to do anything now!" Tom cried, but the mist was fading. "Malvel, I will fight you to the death!" Tom cried, his hands clenched on his sword. The Evil Wizard did not reply. The vision of Hugo and the Golden Knight faded away.

In the silence of the kitchen, the Varkule rose to its feet and growled.

CHAPTER THREE

A PROMISE OF REVENGE

The Varkule launched itself at Elenna's throat. Tom jumped to intercept it with a swing of his sword. *Crash!* He tripped on a broken plate and fell before he could reach the creature. Elenna's arrow whistled overhead, missing the Varkule. As Tom scrambled up, Elenna reached into her quiver for another arrow but

before she could notch it to her bow
the creature's paws slammed into her
chest. She stumbled back towards the
fireplace and the arrow flew from her
hand, skidding from sight.

"I'm coming!" Tom yelled.

Elenna snatched an iron spit from
the hearth as the varkule sprang
again. With all her strength, she
stabbed forwards. The Varkule was
moving too quickly to stop and it was
impaled on the sharp point, piercing

itself through the heart. With a howl of defeat, it fell to the floor and lay still.

"Is it dead?" Elenna asked, breathing hard.

"Let's not take any chances," Tom replied. He raised his sword above his head as he approached the Varkule's body. But when he looked more closely he could see that the creature's flanks weren't moving.

Elenna caught Tom's arm. "Look outside. It's nearly dusk! We're running out of time." A glance at the high windows showed Tom the late afternoon sun.

"'I will expect to be back in Avantia by nightfall,'" he said, repeating Malvel's threat. Elenna was right – there was no time to waste. "If he wants to be here, then let's bring him here. Come on!"

He stormed along the corridor, Elenna close behind him. In the infirmary, Daltec was rearranging feather pillows behind Aduro's head.

"Much too dangerous," Aduro was muttering as Tom entered the room.

Tom leant over the old man's bed while Daltec shrank back against the wall.

"I was just saying this final Quest has grown too dangerous," Aduro repeated to Tom. The wizard's kind face was pale but his eyes were focused.

"I won't abandon my Quest," Tom said. "I will avenge my father and save King Hugo!"

"Save Hugo?" Aduro asked, sitting up in the bed. "Have you had news of him?"

Quickly Elenna explained about the

image the Varkule had brought in the bottle. Aduro sank back onto the bed.

"Look, the afternoon is passing!" Tom gestured. "Aduro, magic Malvel back now. It's the only way to save the king. I'll deal with him when he's here."

"Grief has made you reckless," Aduro cautioned. "If you tackle Malvel in this state, he could defeat you."

"Give me a chance to fight him!" Tom demanded.

"Our king would not wish Avantia to be placed in such danger. I will not summon Malvel back."

Aduro closed his eyes and turned his head away.

"Elenna," Tom muttered, "would you watch over Aduro? Daltec, come and talk to me outside."

Tom tugged Daltec along. With

a kick of his boot, Tom closed the infirmary door. The apprentice's face looked pinched with worry.

"You have done much studying with Aduro," Tom said. "You must know many spells by now."

Daltec gulped and nodded.

"You must use a spell to undo the curse of the Eternal Flame. Bring Malvel back to Avantia."

Daltec gasped in horror. "Malvel is Avantia's greatest threat."

"And Hugo is Avantia's great king. Do you want to be responsible for his death? Now, Daltec! We must act before night falls."

"I'm not sure… Maybe…"

"Come on!" Tom whirled and shoved Daltec up the stairs ahead of him.

In Aduro's chamber, shelves

groaned beneath the weight of hundreds of old books.

"Up here…" Daltec said. He slowly climbed a ladder and pulled books of spells from the shelves.

"The sun is in the western sky," Tom reminded him. "We can't let King Hugo die. Have you found the book yet?"

"Maybe this one," Daltec said, coming down the ladder again. He laid a heavy book on the table and brushed dust off it. "But I don't have the key to open it."

"Stand back," Tom warned. He swung his sword against the book's golden clasp.

Fragments of metal flew off. Daltec opened the covers and fumbled though the parchment pages.

"Here it is," he said at last. Daltec

took a deep breath. He began to
mumble the spell in a quavering
voice:

Knife of Being slice the air,
Summon evil from its lair,
Keep us safe but let us meet,
An enemy brought close to defeat.

Tom lifted his sword high and shifted
into a fighting stance. For a long
moment, nothing happened. Then
a dazzling orange light appeared.

Tom squinted as a ball of flame
exploded in the room. Daltec cried
out and shielded his face from the
intense heat. Like a comet, the ball
shot through the window and left a
trail of smoke. Coughing, Tom rushed
to look out. The comet blazed before
landing in the courtyard below.

As the smoke cleared, Tom saw an anxious ring of servants and guards gathering. In their midst stood a tall thin figure, wrapped in a black cloak with the hood pulled up.

Malvel! Tom thought. *Now I will avenge my father's death!*

CHAPTER FOUR

A QUEST ABANDONED

Malvel flung back his hood. His cunning eyes scanned the courtyard. "Ah, Avantia, now I will be your master!" he said, licking his lips. His mocking laughter echoed off the palace walls. With an upward glance, he saw Tom.

"Seize him!" Tom yelled.

Three soldiers stepped into Malvel's

path but he lifted his wooden staff to shoulder height. Flickers of blue light ran along it. The soldiers fell back, muttering in fear.

"Cowards!" Malvel taunted. Then he disappeared into the stable and the crowd waited to see what would happen next.

A moment later a horse bolted out, with Malvel on its back. The soldiers were knocked aside like bowling pins. The horse's shoes rang on the cobbles, sending up showers of sparks. Its silky black coat blended with the falling shadows. On its forehead gleamed a white mark like an arrowhead.

"Storm!" Tom screamed in despair. He jumped onto the window ledge.

"It's too high – you'll be killed!" Daltec shouted.

Tom swung his shield from his back. Calling on the power of Arcta's feather, he threw himself from the window and soared through the air. The feather token in his shield protected him from falling from great heights. As he landed in the courtyard, Elenna burst out of the castle door. She must have heard the commotion from the infirmary.

"Captain Harkman!" Tom shouted.

"Lower the portcullis!"

As the captain rushed to obey, Tom chased after Malvel. The iron portcullis creaked as it was lowered from the gatehouse. Faster and faster Storm galloped, his eyes rolling white. The Evil Wizard clung to him like a leech. At the last moment, the portcullis slammed to the ground. Storm sank onto his haunches, skidding to a stop. His muzzle banged against the iron bars.

With a cruel twist of the reins, Malvel dragged Storm's head around and trotted him back to Tom.

"You're trapped – give in now!" Tom yelled.

Malvel's icy glare sent shivers down Tom's spine.

"You are only a boy," he said with contempt. "Without your father,

you are nothing. You play at being
a knight in your father's Golden
Armour, but you will never be the
hero that Taladon was. You will never
have his skill and daring."

Malvel's words slammed into Tom's
gut. He staggered back. *He's right*, Tom
thought. *I will never be like Taladon.
If I'd been a better son, maybe my father
wouldn't be dead now.*

Malvel gave a high, chilling laugh.
Storm shied but Malvel steadied him
with a wrench on the bit. Froth hung
from Storm's lips.

"You know something else, boy?"
Malvel continued. "I'm going to teach
you a lesson. I'm going to take away
everything you hold dear. Thank you
for bringing me into Avantia – now
I can truly take my revenge."

The wizard smacked his staff against

Storm's flanks. Blue light flickered over the stallion. Squealing with terror, Storm lurched around and galloped straight at the iron bars of the portcullis.

He's going to kill Storm. Oh no, please not Storm! Tom thought.

Malvel held his staff level. At the last moment, a bolt of lightning shot from it, blasting the portcullis open. Storm leapt through the twisted

metal. His hoof beats thundered away in a cloud of dust.

"Where can Malvel be going?" Captain Harkman asked.

Tom knew. *Errinel. He said he would take away everything I hold dear. Not just Storm, but Uncle Henry and Aunt Maria too. I have to stop him!*

A faint voice sounded from behind Tom's back: "I can help."

Spinning round, Tom saw Aduro tottering over with Daltec supporting him.

The palace physician hustled behind them. "You are too weak for this!" he protested. "You should remain in bed!"

"The kingdom is at stake. I cannot lie in bed," Aduro mumbled. He held out a marble ball in shaking hands – it was the map Tom had carried on this Quest.

In the fading light, Tom leant over the marble ball. A map of Avantia formed on its shiny surface. A thin line showed the journey of the Golden Knight.

"He is heading towards the mountains where Ferno the Fire Dragon lives," Aduro said. "You must stop him from harming Ferno."

"I'm going to Errinel first," Tom said. "My family is in danger." He'd never put his loved ones before a Quest, but since his father had died… *I can't bring more pain and misery to the people I love! I have to stop Malvel!*

"Errinel and the mountains are many miles apart," pointed out Aduro. "You are allowing Malvel to distract you from your Quest. Ferno needs your help."

"And so do my aunt and uncle!" Tom cried, his face hot with anger.

"Take the ball and see which Beast

you must fight next," Aduro urged. "Remember, Tom, the Golden Knight is out there, with our king. There's a danger he could turn into an Evil Beast. Are you prepared to let that happen?" He thrust the marble map into Tom's hands. Reluctantly, Tom peered at the mountains.

"Doomskull," Tom read aloud. "The next Beast is called Doomskull."

What was more important – the Golden Knight in the mountains or the Evil Wizard in his home village?

Tom lifted the marble ball high. It glittered for a moment before Tom flung it savagely down. The ball smashed into a hundred bright fragments on the stones and everyone jumped back with a cry.

"The Quest will have to wait!" Tom shouted defiantly. "I am going after Malvel!"

CHAPTER FIVE

AMBUSHED IN THE CORN

"Elenna," Tom said, "are you with me? I understand if you want to stay here."

Elenna's green eyes glanced uncertainly from the shattered ball, to Tom and then to Aduro.

"I don't have time to waste!" Tom exclaimed and he strode into the stable. In a far stall stood his father's chestnut-coloured horse, Fleetfoot. The stallion's head hung and his eyes were half-closed. *He is mourning too*, Tom realised.

"Faithful Fleetfoot," Tom murmured. "We must ride into battle."

The stallion's eyes opened and light stirred in them. When Tom held up the bridle, Fleetfoot bent his head willingly. Tom flung a saddle over his back and tightened the girth.

"Wait for us," Elenna called from a stall near the door. "I am not letting you face this fight alone." She led Blizzard out, and Silver trotted alongside.

Tom's heart lifted to see his loyal companion joining him once again. He gave her a nod of thanks. "Let's ride!" he said.

The courtyard was empty. Tom and Elenna mounted and the horses sprang forwards. They pounded through the blasted portcullis and settled to a steady gallop. Silver streaked alongside on silent paws.

"Can you see anything ahead?" Elenna asked.

Tom narrowed his eyes above Fleetfoot's whipping mane. He had left the golden helmet by the watering trough, but its powers still worked and he could see far into the distance. A smudge of dust showed where Storm galloped along the path.

"The path bends up ahead," Tom said. "Let's take a shortcut through this cornfield and cut across to the far side of the bend!"

He swung Fleetfoot into the tall, rustling stalks of corn. Blizzard and

Silver followed close to the stallion's heels. The stalks clattered in the breeze like dry bones, making the animals nervous and skittish.

Silver whined and lifted his muzzle, sniffing.

"He smells danger," Elenna warned, halting Blizzard. Tom reined in Fleetfoot. They waited, scanning the swaying corn. It shone pale and gold, like an army of ghosts in the light of the setting sun.

"There!" Tom said, pointing to movement to his right. "What was that?"

"No, over there," Elenna said, pointing to the left.

"Maybe it's just a rabbit," Tom suggested impatiently.

There was a flash in the corn. The horses reared, throwing Tom and

Elenna from their saddles and sending them crashing to the ground.

The Golden Knight loomed over them. In each hand he clutched a golden dagger, forked blades honed to razor-sharp points.

Tom sprang back to his feet in an instant. "I thought you were in the mountains," he said. The knight gave a slow, lazy grin and shook his head. Understanding dawned on Tom. "You changed the map. Aduro is weak and you interfered with his magic." The knight shrugged and anger tore through Tom. If he'd followed Aduro's orders, if he'd headed towards the mountains, he'd have been even further from his Quest. He'd been right to head towards Errinel!

The knight stabbed with a knife. Super-human strength flowed into Tom's golden breastplate and he blocked the blow with his arm. The forked blade glanced off his armour and the force of his counter sent the knight back into a retreat.

"Where's King Hugo?" Tom demanded, his voice low and threatening. The knight threw his head back and laughed. This was Tom's chance! He drew his sword in a single, fluid motion and advanced on the Golden Knight. Seeing Tom's advance, the knight lunged with his own weapons.

"Elenna, keep the horses safe!" Tom cried, reaching for his shield, which still hung from Fleetfoot's saddle.

Step by step, Tom beat the Golden knight back. His sword slashed the air and crashed down on the knight's shoulders. The flat of the blade smacked against the Knight's chest. But his foe fought back, aiming his daggers at Tom's unprotected face. *I should have brought the helmet*, Tom thought.

Over and over he parried the knight's daggers as they slashed at his head. One of Tom's feet tangled in the corn stalks. He struggled to free his foot. *Whoosh!* The point of a dagger scored a cut across Tom's cheek. Blood poured down his neck. With a frantic heave, Tom pulled free of the corn. He ducked under the knight's next swing, beating him back with his shield. The knight's armour rang

under the savage blow.

Anger and desperation surged through Tom, increasing his wild strength. Sweat drenched his back. His muscles burned, but he clenched his teeth and fought on.

Thrashing free of the corn, Tom drove the Golden Knight back towards the shadowy walls of an old barn. Steel rang on steel. Sparks showered from blades. Armour became dented and scratched.

Tom brought his sword high in a slicing arc. The Golden Knight jumped out of range but his heavy armour overbalanced him. *Crash!* He plunged through the barn wall in a cloud of dust. Tom gasped for breath, his side cramping. His vision blurred with fatigue. Where was the Golden Knight?

Strange snarling noises came from the barn. The barn roof shook. Slates crashed to the ground. The walls of the barn shuddered. With a tremendous roar, they collapsed. Tom leapt back as boards and nails rained down.

From the wreckage, a huge form rose – a gigantic Beast! Tom craned his neck, staring in shock. *A stone lion,* he thought. It was alive and heaving with muscle.

The Beast swivelled its skeletal head. Tom saw there was no skin or flesh covering its bones. Massive teeth and sabre-tooth fangs gleamed orange in the wreath of flames around the Beast's neck. Its empty eyes sockets glowed like gold nuggets.

Doomskull!

CHAPTER SIX

THE FANG OF DOOMSKULL

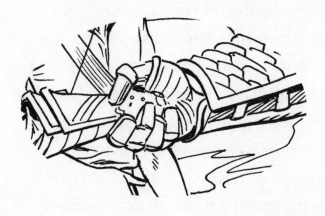

With a roar that shook Tom's chest, Doomskull crouched and then sprang through the air. Before Tom could react, a huge paw smashed into his breastplate. There was a squeal as claws raked down Taladon's armour. Tom flew above the corn and crashed to the ground. His shield spiralled out of sight. Dazed and dizzy, Tom struggled to sit up. Stars swam in his vision. He gasped for breath, swiping the blood trickling from his cheek.

By now, Tom knew that each knight was capable of transforming into a Beast if the battle was turning against them. Tom had so nearly defeated the Golden Knight, but that had just made his enemy turn into Doomskull!

With another roar, the Beast charged to finish Tom off. Arrows bounced from the Beast's stone flanks. *Elenna!* Tom thought. She must have tied the horses up to join in the fight. *She would never leave me. Thank goodness!* Another arrow flew through the air and Doomskull darted aside, stumbling slightly. But he was soon back on all fours, facing Tom, fangs dripping as he opened his mouth in a mighty roar.

Tom lurched to his feet, trying to find his balance. Pushing aside corn stalks, he backed away from Doomskull, then turned and ran across the field in Elenna's direction.

Behind him, Doomskull snarled and crashed through the corn. Tom skidded to a stop and leant, gasping, against Fleetfoot's warm flank. Silver licked his hands while Elenna and Blizzard crowded close.

"What can we do?" Elenna asked. Her lips were set in a firm line. "We're not giving up now." She gripped the horses' reins with white knuckles.

Doomskull appeared behind them in an explosion of shredded leaves and fangs. The Beast swatted Blizzard aside, and she gave a whinny of pain as claws raked her shoulder. Blood splattered her white coat.

Tom jumped between Blizzard and Doomskull, holding up his sword. Without his shield, he felt like a fly waiting to be swatted. He could barely see now, as the day's light faded.

"Where's the token to defeat the final Beast?" Elenna called.

"In Storm's saddle bag!" Tom panted. But Storm was with Malvel. He swung around, holding his sword steady as Doomskull stalked him in the trampled corn. The Beast's whiskers were like strands of glowing wire and its fiery mane blackened nearby corn stalks. *Any moment now, and he'll finish me off*, Tom thought. *Then he'll kill Elenna and the horses.*

"That token in Storm's bag probably couldn't help us anyway!" Elenna called. "It was just a small tooth."

"Perhaps it would have grown

bigger when I used it," Tom
wondered. "Like the harpoon I
used against Voltrex in the Western
Ocean."

The tip of Tom's sword wavered.
His arms were exhausted. *I can't hold
the Beast at bay much longer.*

Doomskull snarled, his lips
wrinkling back over his drooling
fangs.

Of course! Tom thought. "Maybe I can
use one of Doomskull's own fangs," he
shouted. It had to be worth a try. He
tensed his leg muscles and then, with
a mighty kick, Tom sprang into the air.
The power of the golden boots sent
him flying in a high somersault. He
whistled towards Doomskull's skeletal
face. With a swinging blow, he hacked
at one of the Beast's fangs – his sword
sank into the gum. Doomskull's roar of

pain nearly split Tom's eardrums. Tom
wrenched at his sword and the tooth
spun through the air to land at Elenna's
feet. She quickly scooped it up.

The creature snapped at Tom, but
he launched himself backwards and
landed on the ground beside Elenna.
"I don't know...if this will work," he

gasped. "Give me the fang."

Tom wielded the slick, smooth fang in both hands like a broadsword. It was nearly as long as his blade and it curved to a razor-sharp tip that gleamed. As Doomskull leapt in fury, Tom aimed the point of the fang at the throat of the great creature. Doomskull smashed down onto it with a blow that made the ground shudder. Tom felt the Beast's weight impaled on the fang and the lion's mane brushed against his skin. Tom was almost crushed as the Beast crumpled to the ground, but he rolled aside and jumped to his feet. Had his plan worked?

Doomskull's flames flickered and died. The golden glow in his empty eye sockets faded. With a final crash, Doomskull toppled and lay still, gleaming in the starlight. Then he began to fade until he vanished altogether.

In the Beast's place, the outline of a man in armour began to form, limbs twitching. Then the Golden Knight arose from the ground and faced Tom. "Thank you for freeing me from Malvel's curse," he said. "I must return to my resting place in the Gallery of Tombs."

Tom felt some of the anger in his heart melting away. He held out a hand and the knight's armoured hand closed around his fingers. He gave a short, strong shake.

"I know the evil didn't come from you," Tom said. The knight bent his head in acknowledgement.

"I shall feel the stain of Malvel on my soul forever," the knight muttered. "My reputation lies in tatters."

"That's not true!" Tom gasped,

though part of him understood how
the knight felt. He'd felt his own
worth crumble away at his father's
death. But if the Golden Knight could
be returned to his rightful place with
honour…did that mean that Avantia's
king would feel proud of Tom again?

"Where's King Hugo?" Tom asked
quickly. "You were holding him hostage!"

The knight passed a hand across his brow. "I think… I believe… I'm not sure, but I think Aduro found the strength to magic him back to the palace." He looked around. "He's not here. Have faith. He may even now be back on his throne." The image of the knight began to fade away. "I must go now…" The outline of his armour disappeared to a dot and then nothing. Tom and Elenna were alone.

Tom turned to Fleetfoot. The brave stallion had waited close by, sweating with fear. Tom leapt onto his back.

"What are you doing?" Elenna asked. "You haven't found your shield yet – you can't go without it."

"I have no choice. I have to find Malvel. He might be in Errinel already, harming my aunt and uncle!"

"But Tom, you can't leave your

shield!" she gasped.

"Will you look for it?" he asked. "Use it to heal Blizzard's wounds."

"You're not going without me, Tom!" Elenna said, folding her arms.

Tom wasn't sure how to choose the right words. "What I'm doing next is personal. I can't get you involved. King Hugo is safe and so is Avantia. Now, I want my revenge on Malvel."

Elenna looked shocked. Her mouth gaped and her green eyes stretched. "You can't be serious!"

"I mean it," Tom said "This next fight is mine alone."

"No, Tom! Please let me come— "

Tom couldn't stop to think. *The fight is mine alone!* He nudged Fleetfoot into a gallop. Elenna's cries faded in the distance. The last thing Tom heard was Silver howling.

CHAPTER SEVEN

FATE OF THE INNOCENT

Even with magical vision, Tom saw
nothing ahead. The path stretched
empty in the light of the full moon.
Too late, I'm too late. In desperation,
he stroked Fleetfoot's sweating neck
and urged the horse to go faster. As
they approached Errinel, the stallion
pounded through a wheat field that
Tom recognized. He and Uncle Henry

had once flown a kite here.

As Fleetfoot entered the streets of Errinel, everything seemed wrong. Where was the warm flicker of candlelight in the windows? Houses stood dark with their doors barred. Not a single person was about and even the dogs were silent. Tom's heart hammered hard in his chest. He urged Fleetfoot toward the village square. In its centre stood a figure. A tall, thin figure wrapped in a dark cloak and hood. *Malvel!*

And at his feet... *Oh no!* Tom thought.

"Let them go! They are innocent!" he shouted.

As Fleetfoot skidded to a halt, Uncle Henry and Aunt Maria looked up. Their faces were taut with terror. Shoulder to shoulder, they kneeled

before Malvel, bound tightly by magical bonds of glowing light. Over their heads, Malvel waved his staff.

"Welcome, Tom!" Malvel gave a twisted smile. "You are just in time to watch the sad remains of your family meet their death. Just like your father."

"Never!" Tom cried in defiance.

"These good people have done nothing to deserve this."

"Ride away, Tom," Uncle Henry commanded. "You must save yourself."

"Leave us here," Aunt Maria croaked. "Escape while you still can!"

"I won't leave you!" Tom said, dismounting from Fleetfoot. He advanced upon Malvel, drawing his sword. The wizard aimed the staff tip at Tom's heart and growled like a dog.

"You are the cause of all my suffering!" Tom said through gritted teeth.

"Fight me and I'll end your suffering forever!" Malvel sneered. Suddenly, Malvel's eyes widened.

Tom spun around to see what the wizard was looking at. From out of the darkness, six knights stalked forward in chilling silence. Moonlight gleamed on the colours of their shining helmets and breastplates: red, blue, gold, white, black and silver.

"The Knights of Forton!" Tom gasped. Hairs stood up on his arms.

"Attack that miserable wretch Tom!" Malvel commanded the knights. His voice was high and tight with fear. The knights carried on marching, not towards Tom, but towards the Evil Wizard.

"Slay him!" Malvel cried, pointing a quivering finger at Tom.

Nothing. The knights kept up their silent advance and Malvel began to back away.

"The curse on them truly has lifted," Tom gasped in relief. He strode across to his aunt and uncle. "The knights' hearts are good again. They've come

to help!" He hooked an arm beneath
his aunt's elbow and raised her to her
feet. Beside her, Uncle Henry stiffly
straightened up.

"Go! Take cover!" Tom told them.

They ran towards the forge.

The knights drew their fearsome weapons. Moonlight glinted on an axe, a sword, a flail and twin daggers. The points of a lance and a mace gleamed. Uneasily, Malvel backed farther away. Fear flickered over his face. Tom thought that Malvel was going to admit defeat. Then suddenly his eyes glittered with cold malice.

"You have underestimated me, Tom," he hissed. "You all have."

The knights rushed forwards to attack. Malvel muttered a spell. He threw up his hands and silver bolts surrounded each of the Knights. Held in place, they could only glare at the wizard from the edges of the square. Tom tried to advance on Malvel, but he felt his own body fixed to the ground.

I can't move! I can't do anything to help!
Tom thought.

"I'll fight you one at a time," Malvel cackled. He said another spell and the staff in his hand hardened from wood into a silver fighting pole. Its long, hard length glittered in the moonlight. Each end tapered to a deadly point.

"Red, you first."

At Malvel's command, the Red Knight advanced, released from the silver bolt. Tom watched, holding his breath. Malvel raised his pole high and easily parried the knight's sword thrusts. He smashed the pole down against the knight's sword and almost knocked it from his hands

Tom watched Malvel fight. Already, the Red Knight sprawled motionless on the ground. Malvel released the

White Knight to advance into the centre of the square. The knight gripped his lance in both hands and raised it high like a fighting staff. He and Malvel leapt together, their staves ringing. Malvel's staff spun in the air, creating circles, clover leaves and figure-eight's. Finally, Malvel jabbed forward. His staff thudded into the knight's forehead. A red hole blossomed. The knight keeled backwards and lay still.

Was the great knight defeated?

CHAPTER EIGHT

A WARRIOR'S DEATH

The knight groaned and rolled over onto his side, before pulling himself along the ground to rest against a tree trunk.

These men are brave, Tom thought. *Surely Malvel won't beat them all!* If only he could do something to help.

One by one, the knights advanced. The wizard leapt, spun, cartwheeled and kicked. His robe flapped and his staff twirled. *He's like a windmill in a storm,* Tom thought. *There's no stopping him.*

Malvel dodged the Blue Knight's swinging mace. His staff smashed the knight's hand and he dropped his weapon with a howl of pain. Malvel was a blur, striking the Blue Knight to the ground.

The Golden Knight's forked daggers were too short to slip beneath Malvel's guard. The knight crouched and circled, searching for an opening beneath Malvel's staff. Suddenly, Malvel lunged and knocked the daggers onto the ground. The sharp tip of his staff pierced the knight's heart. Tom groaned.

Now it was the Black Knight's turn. *He must beat Malvel!* Tom thought. He clenched his fists. His hopes were

ebbing away but his anger was still
rising.

Malvel twirled his staff against the
swinging chains of the Black Knight's
flail. Jumping back, he wrenched
the flail from the knight's grip. With
a corkscrew of his staff, he flung the
flail across the square. Using a high,
spinning kick, Malvel knocked the
knight down.

"You're the last one. Come on! You can defeat Malvel!" Tom shouted as the Silver Knight stepped forwards. The edges of his double-headed axe gleamed. He circled the wizard, then struck... His axe head disappeared into the wizard's black robe.

Yes, Malvel's been hit! Is he wounded? Tom waited.

Malvel retreated, snarling. The knight threw his axe at the wizard's back. At the last moment, the wizard snatched the weapon from the air and hurled it back at the knight. It sank into his chest and the knight crashed down.

Tom stood stunned. The knights lay strewn around the square. His mouth felt dry. He licked his lips. "It is my turn to fight you now! Release me." Tom gripped the hilt of his

sword. Malvel snapped his fingers
and Tom was released. "For Taladon
and Avantia!" he cried, running
forwards. With a mighty swing of
his sword, Tom lunged at Malvel.
The wizard's staff snapped up and
hit Tom in the stomach. The force of
the impact rocked Tom back on his
heels. Malvel's staff swung in a circle.
The tip thrust in, quick as a snake
bite, and rang against Tom's shoulder.
Tom staggered. Malvel pressed his

advantage. He lifted his staff to shoulder height in both hands and slammed its length across Tom's chest. Taladon's golden armour buckled.

Tom reared up on a wave of rage. He had no shield and he could see that Malvel was a formidable enemy, but through his anger he felt the surge of power that Taladon's magical gauntlets gave him. Using his special sword skills, Tom hacked and swung at Malvel, pressing the wizard back across the cobblestones. Steel rang on steel. Armour groaned and buckled. Malvel's hissing laughter coiled around them.

The moon rose high over the village square. Malvel and Tom circled, crouched, jumped, lashed out and parried. Malvel's eyes gleamed like white stones. His staff struck like silver lightning.

Suddenly, as Tom raised his sword, Malvel's staff darted in low and whacked him across the knee. Tom staggered. Malvel's staff swung around and the point jabbed Tom in the stomach. Breath whooshed from him. Darkness flooded his eyes. He toppled over with a thud that made his head spin.

"Give up now!" Malvel cackled.

With a grimace, Tom found his voice. "I will never give up. Not while there is blood in my veins," he croaked.

"Boy, there won't be blood in your veins for much longer," Malvel cried.

As Tom climbed shakily to his feet, Malvel lunged, smashing his staff down again and again on Tom's armour. It cracked and scratched. Tom tried to lift his sword, but one furious swing of Malvel's staff knocked it from his hand. The sword clattered to the ground. Tom swayed. His ears roared. His head spun with fatigue.

This is the end, Tom thought.

Malvel leapt into the air and kicked Tom in the chest. He fell back with a crash of armour and lay as still as the defeated knights.

"What a pathetic excuse for a warrior," Malvel said. "You're just a snivelling boy."

The wizard picked up Tom's sword.

The sword that Aduro gave me for my Quest, Tom thought.

Tom moaned. He was too exhausted even to stand up. Blood trickled down his neck. His hair was plastered to his forehead. Every muscle in his body burned. With foggy vision, Tom

watched Malvel raise his staff high.

"People of Errinel!" Malvel shrieked
in triumph. "Come and witness the
end of your so-called champion. He
wanted to be a warrior. I give him
a warrior's death!"

CHAPTER NINE

THE GHOST'S SWORD

"Tom, get on your feet!"

Tom groaned, his eyes still closed. *I'm hearing voices now. I must be almost dead.*

"Tom, get up." The voice in Tom's ears was firm and kind, and it sounded familiar.

"Tom, my dear son, get up."

Father? Tom's eyes jerked open.

A faint image of Taladon leant over Tom. He gave a smile that brought warmth to Tom's chilled bones.

"Have you already forgotten my final words?" Taladon asked.

Tom's tongue moved slowly, thick in his dry mouth. "No, Father. You said, 'the Quest continues'."

Taladon nodded and reached to the scabbard hanging at his side. He pulled out a ghostly sword and held it towards Tom.

"I can't fight any longer," Tom whispered.

"Who are you talking to, you little worm?" Malvel demanded, striding over the cobbles.

"Take my sword, Tom," Taladon urged. His image wavered. Weakly, Tom held out one bruised hand, in which Taladon laid the sword. As

soon as Tom curled his fingers around
it, the sword became real. It was cold,
shining and heavy. Amazing strength
rushed from it and through Tom's
body. His head and his vision cleared.

"The Quest continues!" he said.

For a moment, he saw the pride in

Taladon's eyes. Then the image faded. Tom jumped to his feet and held Taladon's sword high. Moonlight ran along the blade like white fire.

"What magic is this?" Malvel exclaimed. His mouth gaped and he reeled back.

"This is not magic – this is my destiny!" Tom cried. "I will defeat you at last!"

Again, the two of them circled the square, stepping between the fallen knights. Malvel held Tom's old sword in one hand and his staff in the other. He sliced sideways with the sword. Tom raised Taladon's weapon and easily blocked Malvel's move. Malvel jumped. From the whirl of his robes, the sword and the staff lunged towards Tom in a spinning blur. Tom flung up Taladon's sword again. He knocked his own sword from Malvel's hand with a sharp ring. It landed on the cobbles and skidded into the shadows.

Now Malvel concentrated on using his staff. He swung it sideways against Tom's ankles, trying to knock Tom from his feet. Tom jumped high into the air then brought Taladon's sword down in a smashing blow. The force of the impact on the staff shook Tom's shoulders, but he hacked it into two pieces!

Malvel fell backwards onto the stones. Tom straddled him and raised his father's sword to shoulder-height, gripping it in both hands. The tip was aimed at Malvel's throat.

"Prepare to die," Tom said through gritted teeth. The Evil Wizard writhed between Tom's feet, babbling and weeping, covering his face with his hands.

"Have mercy on me," he cried, biting his lips until they bled. "Young Tom, show mercy."

"Quiet!" Tom shouted. He clenched his fingers around Taladon's sword. In a moment, it would all be over – Tom would never have to fight this old enemy again.

The sword point wavered. Malvel opened one eye.

Tom's anger drained away. *Another death will not bring my father back,* he thought.

Tom lowered his weapon. "I have proved myself countless times against you," he said. "I do not need to kill you to be a hero. I will not spill blood with my father's sword."

Gasps of astonishment echoed in

the square. Lifting his head, Tom saw
that the villagers had crept outside in
silence.

"That's my boy!" Uncle Henry's

proud smile shone in the moonlight.

Taladon's sword and Golden Armour suddenly vanished from Tom. They had served their purpose.

"King Hugo will decide Malvel's fate," Tom told the people of Errinel. "Bring ropes to bind him. He shall be taken to the palace dungeons to await his punishment."

The crowd parted to let through a villager carrying a coil of rope. Tom stepped forward to take it, but there was a sudden scrambling noise behind him.

"Look out!" Aunt Maria loudly shrieked.

Tom whirled around as Malvel jumped from the ground. He launched himself towards Tom. One hand was upraised, clenching a dagger he'd pulled from his robe.

At that moment, a great shadow blotted out the moonlight and the village square plunged into darkness.

CHAPTER TEN

A NEW BEAST MASTER

Massive wings whooshed overhead.
Wind beat against Tom's face. *What
is happening? Is this some new magic
of Malvel's? I must find my sword!* he
thought.

Tom had never been on a Quest
that seemed so never-ending.
Moonlight spilled over the square.
He looked up and saw the mighty
silhouette of a Beast with leathery

wings and a spiked black head. It
was Ferno!

"You've come to help!" Tom cried.
There, crouched on the dragon's back,
was Elenna, carrying Tom's shield.
She must have called to the Beast,
hoping that Ferno would hear her all
the way from the mountains. He was
the last Beast to join them on this
Quest.

Swooping lower, Ferno opened
his mouth. Tom saw the red bank of
embers sizzling inside. Heat poured
over Tom and flapped Malvel's robes.

"This is the end of your evil!"
Elenna shouted, her face a grim
mask between the dragon's shoulders.
Malvel shrieked in fear. His dagger
fell with a clatter as he flung his
arm across his face. Flames shot
from the dragon's mouth and villagers

rushed away, screaming.

Tom crouched in a doorway. Heat
beat against him, singeing his hair. He
squeezed his eyes shut. A stench of
burning reeked in Tom's nostrils and

a terrible shrieking rang in his ears.

Then, silence.

Tom shakily rose to his feet.
The square was empty except for a
blackened dagger. Wisps of burned
robe drifted nearby like ashes. Malvel
was gone. All that was left of him was
a pile of charred clothes.

"Thank you, Ferno!" Tom shouted
as the dragon swooped in to land on
the cobblestones. Villagers rushed
back into the square. Tom was
grabbed and swept into a tight hug
by Aunt Maria and Uncle Henry.
When Elenna arrived, they put their
arms around her too. For a long
moment, the four of them stood
locked together, dizzy with joyful
relief. Silver scampered around them,
anxious to be let into the group.
They pulled apart, laughing.

"First I found your shield, Tom, and then I found Ferno," Elenna said. "He seemed to know what was needed."

"I can't believe you rode on the dragon's back!" Tom exclaimed. "Thank you. You saved my life. Did you heal Blizzard too?" As Tom spoke, the villagers surged apart. Three horses galloped into the square, snorting, their hooves ringing, their bits jingling. They skidded to a stop by Elenna and Tom.

"You did heal Blizzard!" Tom cried in delight, patting the white mare's neck. "And Fleetfoot is safe. And Storm – oh, Storm! I've been so worried about you!" Tom put his arms around the stallion's black head. The horse pressed his face to Tom's chest and nuzzled his hands. Tom gazed from face to happy face.

He turned to Elenna. "We've done it. We've really done it," he said, shaking his head.

His friend smiled. "Taladon would have been proud of you," she said.

She'd chosen the perfect words.

The pink light of dawn broke over the rooftops. Suddenly, in a chicken coop, feathers flew and hens cackled. Tom retrieved his sword and shield. Storm trotted beside him as he ran towards the coop. He was just in time to see Aduro, Daltec, and King Hugo climb out of the coop, brushing feathers from their clothes.

"Daltec still has to work on his transportation spells," Aduro muttered. Tom suppressed a smile and plucked a feather from the Good

Wizard's tangled grey hair. He seemed much better now.

"Malvel is gone!" Tom announced. Two pairs of eyes widened in astonishment, though Aduro didn't seem as surprised. "Come and see for yourselves!"

The men followed as Tom led them into the square where they paced around Malvel's ashy remains.

"Can this be true?" King Hugo asked. "Are we at last free of the Evil Wizard? Is Avantia saved?"

Aduro nodded. His grey eyes twinkled. "I can sense that it is truly over," he agreed. "Thanks to Tom and Elenna!"

"Don't forget the animals: Storm and Silver, Fleetfoot and Blizzard!" Elenna said.

Aduro's eyes twinkled brighter

and the king smiled.

"But I almost failed my Quest," Tom said. "Anger got control of me. I let Malvel loose in the kingdom."

"You were grief-stricken about your father's death," Aduro said gently. "But you gave up your anger and made the right choice. You decided not to spill blood. I was watching from afar. I saw the difficult decisions you had to make."

"You have proved yourself a true warrior," King Hugo said.

"Now the Knights of Forton will sleep safely in their tombs for eternity," Aduro said. He waved a hand across the square, and the knights' bodies lifted up into the air. Then, with a flash of light, they were gone. "A period of hope and prosperity will befall the kingdom."

"Kneel, Tom," commanded King Hugo.

Villagers formed a respectful circle as their tall king, in his green silk robe, pulled his sword from its jewelled sheath.

King Hugo touched Tom's shoulder with the sword tip. "From this moment on you will be Master of the Beasts."

Master of the Beasts! Tom felt a thrill of surprise and delight. *This is a greater honour than I ever dreamed of!*

"And Elenna," King Hugo continued, "you will be known as Faithful Companion to Avantia's Master of the Beasts. You have fought with courage."

King Hugo placed a circlet of silver on Elenna's dark hair.

"Stand to your feet and hold your

head high, Tom," the king said. "You have fought as valiantly as your father ever did."

Tom rose and stood shoulder

to shoulder with Elenna. In the background, Ferno let out small streams of smoke. Villagers cheered and the horses whinnied. Silver pressed close to Elenna, looking up at her. King Hugo's wide smile and Aduro's warm eyes filled Tom with joy. He linked his arm through Elenna's.

"We did it!" she said. "This is the end of our Quest!"

Tom felt a presence standing against his other shoulder. He turned but no one was there. No one he could see, at least. *Father? Thank you for your help.* The air seemed to lighten.

"Evil never rests," Tom told Elenna, turning back to face her. "There will be more Quests for us to face. But for now, Avantia is safe and Malvel is gone for good. His reign of fear is over."

Join Tom in The New Age,
his next Beast Quest adventure
where he will face

ELKO
LORD OF THE SEA

Win an exclusive
Beast Quest T-shirt and goody bag!

Tom has battled many fearsome Beasts and we want to know which one is your favourite! Send us a drawing or painting of your favourite Beast and tell us in 30 words why you think it's the best.

Each month we will select **three** winners to receive a Beast Quest T-shirt and goody bag!

Send your entry on a postcard to
BEAST QUEST COMPETITION
Orchard Books, 338 Euston Road, London NW1 3BH.

Australian readers should email:
childrens.books@hachette.com.au

New Zealand readers should write to:
Beast Quest Competition, PO Box 3255, Shortland St,
Auckland 1140, NZ or email: childrensbooks@hachette.co.nz

**Don't forget to include your name and address.
Only one entry per child.**

Good luck!

Fight the Beasts,
Fear the Magic

www.beastquest.co.uk

Have you checked out the Beast Quest website?
It's the place to go for games, downloads, activities,
sneak previews and lots of fun!

You can read all about your favourite beasts,
download free screensavers and desktop wallpapers
for your computer, and even challenge your friends
to a Beast Tournament.

Sign up to the newsletter at www.beastquest.co.uk
to receive exclusive extra content and the
opportunity to enter special members-only
competitions. We'll send you up-to-date info on all
the Beast Quest books, including the next exciting
series which features four brand-new Beasts!

Beast Quest

All books priced at £4.99,
special bumper editions
priced at £5.99.

Orchard Books are available from all good bookshops, or can
be ordered from our website: www.orchardbooks.co.uk,
or telephone 01235 827702, or fax 01235 8227703.

FREE COLLECTOR CARDS INSIDE!

Series 10: MASTER OF THE BEASTS
COLLECT THEM ALL!

An old enemy has come back to haunt Tom –
and unleash six awesome new Beasts!

978 1 40831 518 7

978 1 40831 519 4

978 1 40831 520 0

978 1 40831 521 7

978 1 40831 522 4

978 1 40831 523 1

Series 11: THE NEW AGE
Out September 2012

Meet six terrifying new Beasts!

Elko Lord of the Sea
Tarrok the Blood Spike
Brutus the Hound of Horror
Flaymar the Scorched Blaze
Serpio the Slithering Shadow
Tauron the Pounding Fury

**Watch out for the next
Special Bumper
Edition
OUT OCT 2012!**